NOTHING MAKES YOU SMILE LIKE A

PURPLE CROCODILE

By Jim Deakins

Illustrations by A. Len Bell

Acknowledgments

First and foremost, I want to thank my precious Granddaughter Gabrielle for her inspiration for this wonderful project. I would also like to thank my niece Meaghan Deakins Fuller for introducing me to the illustrator of the book, A. Len Bell, to Denise Mcdonald, the designer of this book and lastly, to Whitey Schmidt, The Crab Guru, who sadly passed away shortly before the release. None of this would be possible without Whitey, I miss you my friend!

Mr. Deakins plans to donate a large portion of the profits from this book and many hours and years of his time to the St. Jude Children's Hospital and Children's Hospital's across the nation and the National Coalition Against Domestic Violence and several other efforts to prevent violence against women and efforts to benefit children whom are less fortunate.

ISBN 978-0-9908388-0-7

Published by
MURIEL PRESS, LLC
PO Box 85
Fort Walton Beach, FL 32549
mypurplecrocodile.com

Printed in the United States of America

The sign on the side of the road said, "Welcome to the Sunshine State," but little Gabrielle didn't feel like any state of sunshine except extra cloudy with an extra helping of tropical storm on top.

Gabrielle's family was moving to Florida and she didn't know anything about Florida except that it was far way from her old house in her old neighborhood and her old school and all of her friends.

Gabrielle's family was very happy with their new house, but Gabrielle just moped around feeling very sorry for herself.

Her parents wanted to make her feel really happy so they told her about their surprise for her.

"Gabrielle," said her father. "We want you to be really really happy, so we've decided that since we have a yard with our new house, you can have any pet in the whole wide world."

"Any pet?" asked Gabrielle.

"Anything that will make you happy," advised her father.

"Any pet in the whole wide world," repeated her mother. Gabrielle felt just a little bit excited and she asked, "What kind of pet do you think I should get?"

Gabrielle didn't know what to think. At her old house in her old neighborhood she could never have a pet because her family lived in a very small apartment where pets were not allowed, so Gabrielle went to sit on the pier in her new neighborhood and think about what would be the perfect pet.

She thought and thought.

She thought standing up and sitting down.

She thought spinning around.

"WHAT KIND OF PET
WOULD REALLY MAKE
ME SMILE?"

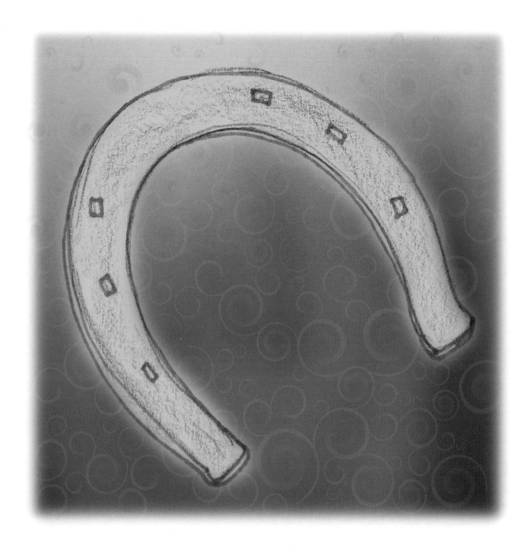

She thought very quietly and finally very loud,

"I would love to have a pony!" She proclaimed, till she thought of a pony living in her little yard and she really didn't know how to take care of a pony.

"Hmmm," she thought. "I would love to have a puppy!"

But then she thought about a kitten and she just couldn't decide between the two.

It seemed like every pet Gabrielle thought about just wasn't quite right, so she just sat on the pier and looked at the beautiful water and said, "I really wish I could think of the perfect pet for me," and at that very instant, a gorgeous Purple Crocodile sprang up from under the pier!

"WOW! YOU'RE BEAUTIFUL!" Gabrielle exclaimed.

She had never seen a Purple Crocodile before but she was sure it was the most gorgeous creature on Earth.

"**C**ould you be my pet?" Gabrielle asked, after all that is what she had been wishing for, and the crocodile battered her eyelashes and said,

"Better yet, we can be best friends!"

So Gabrielle ran home as fast as she could to tell her mother and father she had found the perfect thing to make her the happiest little girl in Florida.

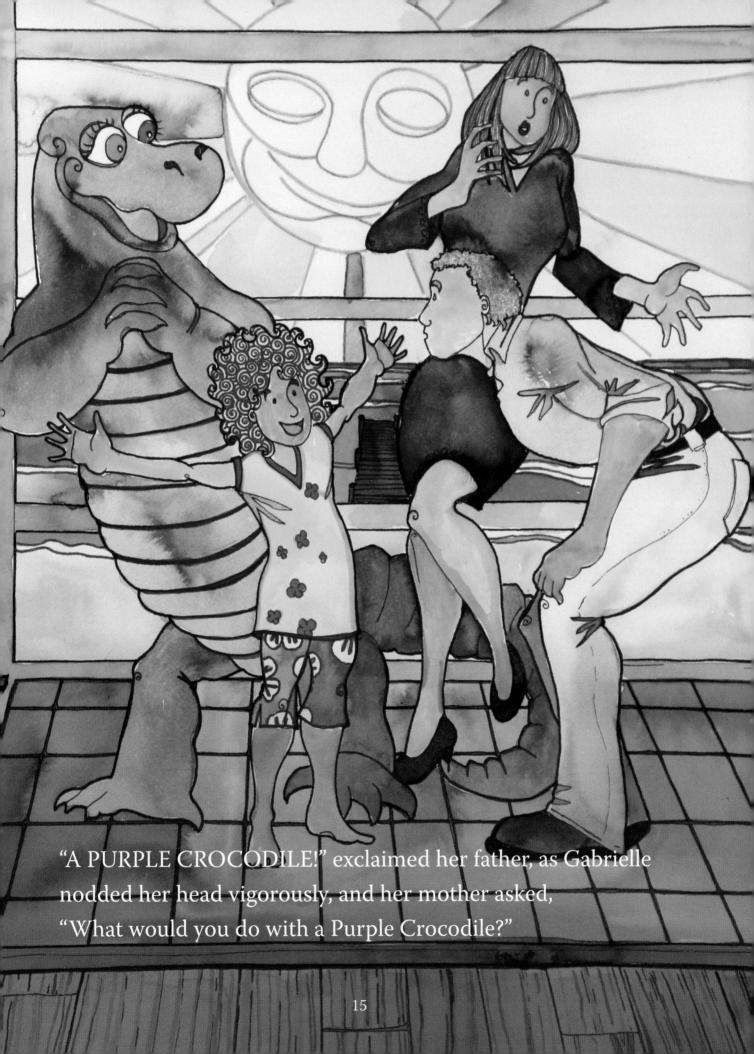

"A PURPLE CROCODILE!" exclaimed her father, as Gabrielle
nodded her head vigorously, and her mother asked,
"What would you do with a Purple Crocodile?"

So Gabrielle says,

"**W**ell, if I had a Purple
Crocodile, it would really
make me smile!

I could take it to school
and show
all my friends!"

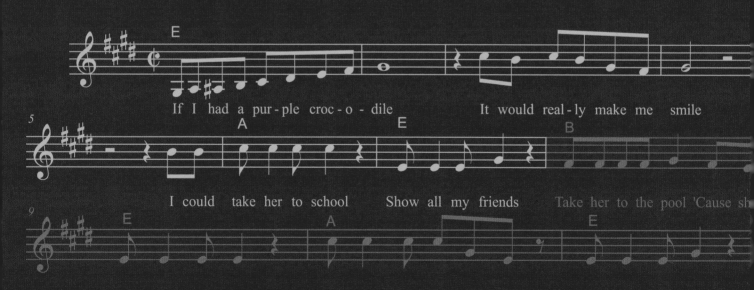

If I had a pur-ple croc-o-dile   It would real-ly make me   smile

I could   take her to school   Show all my friends   Take her to the pool 'Cause sh

"**T**ake her to the pool 'cause she knows how to swim!

Jump off the diving board and splash all the boys!

If I had a Purple Crocodile!"

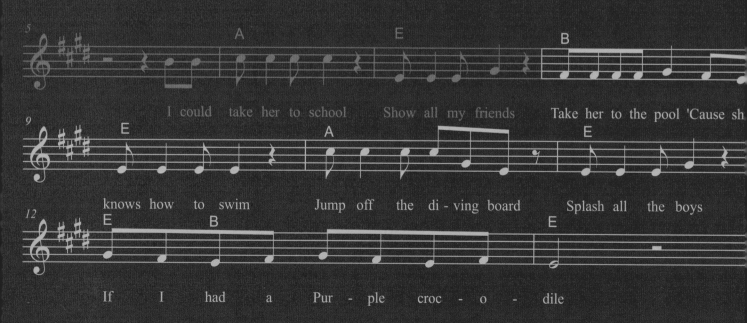

"If I had a Purple Crocodile,

It would really make me smile,

We could jump on the

trampoline ..."

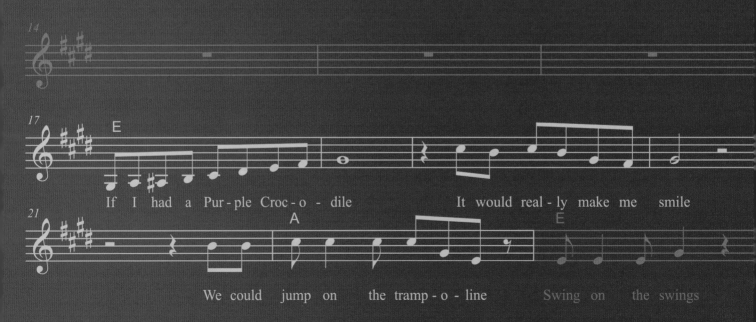

"... and swing on the swings.

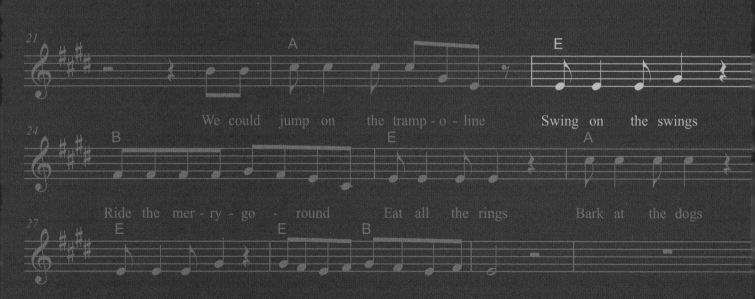

We could jump on the tramp-o-line   Swing on the swings

Ride the mer-ry-go - round   Eat all the rings   Bark at the dogs

"**R**ide the merry go round,

Eat all the rings.

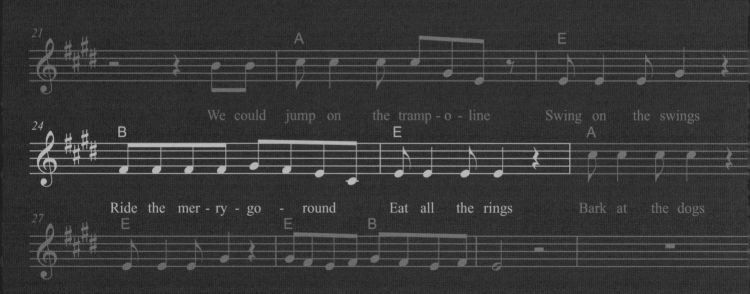

We could jump on the tramp - o - line   Swing on   the swings

Ride the mer - ry - go - round   Eat all   the rings   Bark at   the dogs

"**B**ark at the dogs,
catch purple frogs.

If I had a purple crocodile!"

"If I had a Purple Crocodile,

It would really make me smile!

We could get some roller skates
and go to the park,

Skate all night 'cause she
glows in the dark!

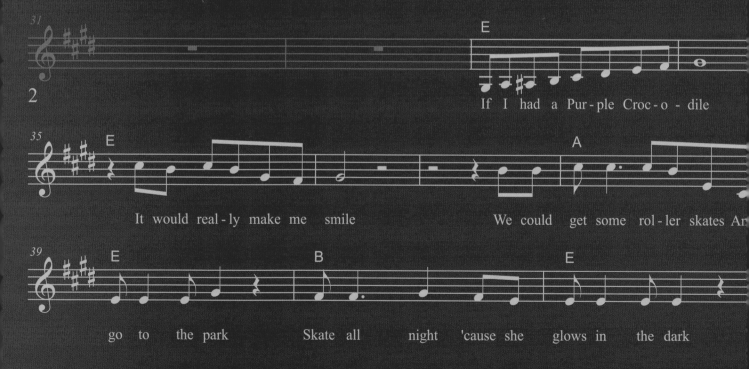

If I had a Pur-ple Croc-o-dile

It would real-ly make me smile   We could   get some rol-ler skates An

go to   the park   Skate all   night 'cause she   glows in   the dark

"**R**ide the ferris wheel
way up high.

If I had a purple crocodile!"

Ride in the Fer-ris wheel   way up   high   If I had a Pur-ple Croc-o-dile

If I had a Pur-ple Cro-co-dile   It would real-ly make me   smile

"If I had a Purple Crocodile,
It would really make me smile!

We could get our paddle boards
and go to the beach,

Chase the dolphins just out of reach.

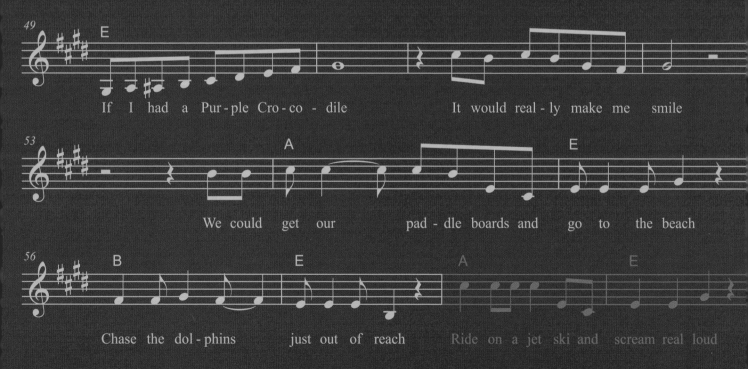

If I had a Pur-ple Cro-co-dile It would real-ly make me smile

We could get our pad-dle boards and go to the beach

Chase the dol-phins just out of reach Ride on a jet ski and scream real loud

"**R**ide on a Jet ski and
scream real loud!

If I had a Purple Crocodile!"

In the end, I met lots of new friends in my new school and my new neighborhood and they loved to come to my new house and meet the Purple Crocodile. I wrote to all of my old friends in my old school and old neighborhood about how sad I was to leave them but how I would never have found my Purple Crocodile if I hadn't.

So, the next time you feel really sad, just imagine the perfect pet who is your best friend and you'll always keep a smile on your face when you have to meet new friends, or go to new places, or do new things you never imagined before! Just find your own Purple Crocodile and keep a really big smile on your face!

The End

A portion of the
profits from this
song and book
will help fight
domestic violence.

Jim Deakins, AUTHOR

Jim has run very successful mortgage businesses for over 20 years, but his true love has always been his guitar playing and songwriting.

In 2000, his daughter suffered a brutal case of domestic violence and Jim was lucky to be in a position to take his daughter and then 2 year old granddaughter in under his wing.

Jim became not only Gabrielle's grandfather but the only father figure that she had. Jim spent many glorious years driving Gabrielle to all sorts of places and while in the car Gabrielle would love to play "I spy with my little eyes". After a couple years of this game Jim became bored with it and made up a game that they played everyday called The Finger Game. Jim would reach back to the car seat and hold Gabrielle's finger and give her two letters, the first being a color and the second being an animal, (i.e. B.D. = blue dog, R.C. = red cat etc). Gabrielle would not get her finger back until she solved the puzzle and then would hold Jim's finger and give him 2 letters, Jim would not get his finger back until he solved the puzzle. Gabrielle soon became very good at this game and one day stumped her grandfather when she announced, P.C.! Jim remembers looking into the rear view mirror and seeing the excitement grow in Gabrielle's face as he could not solve it and Gabrielle blurted out, Purple Crocodile! Thus the Purple Crocodile was born! Purple Crocodile became the go to word and password for everything! One day while waiting for mommy to pick up Gabrielle on her way home from work, Jim and Gabrielle wrote the song, PURPLE CROCODILE which eventually led to Jim writing his first book, *Nothing Makes You Smile Like a Purple Crocodile!*

Jim plans on donating a portion of the profits from this song and book to help fight domestic violence.

A. Len Bell, ILLUSTRATOR

Inspired by his multicultural ancestry, artist and illustrator A. Len Bell traveled the world, exploring and studying cultures and searching for commonalities between them, particularly in language and arts.

He served in several branches of government while continuing his artistic endeavors before meeting his wife Heather. After he retired, they established Loime Studios where they actively inspire each other with their respective artistic talents. Together they homeschool their children Liam and Norá in Baltimore, MD and enjoy exploring the waterways of the Chesapeake Bay, entertaining at their home and planning travels to foreign lands.

Len divides his artistic focus between creating contemporary shaman masks and bowls and illustrating adult and children's literature. His work can be seen through RAW: Natural Born Artists and at www.loimestudios.org and other social media sites.